A Day for Love

by Jill L. Haney

SADDLEBACK
EDUCATIONAL PUBLISHING
www.sdlback.com

ISBN-13: 978-1-62250-851-8
ISBN-10: 1-62250-851-3

Printed in Guangzhou, China
NOR/0814/CA21401334

18 17 16 15 14   1 2 3 4 5

You know the day is near. How?
You see **hearts.**

They are everywhere.
In windows. In stores. On TV.

3

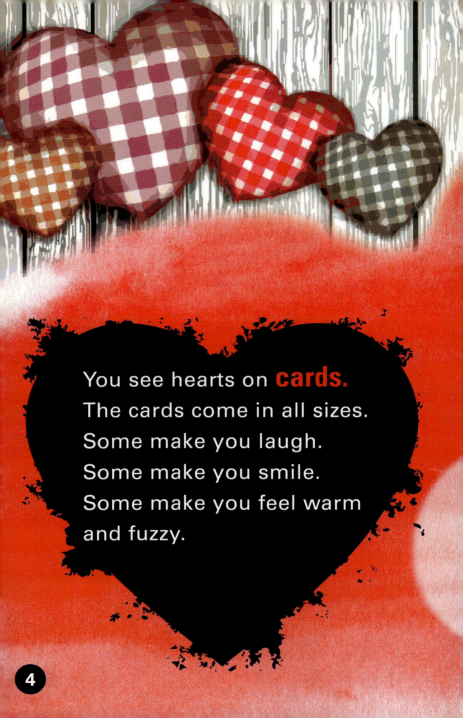

You see hearts on **cards.**
The cards come in all sizes.
Some make you laugh.
Some make you smile.
Some make you feel warm
and fuzzy.

4

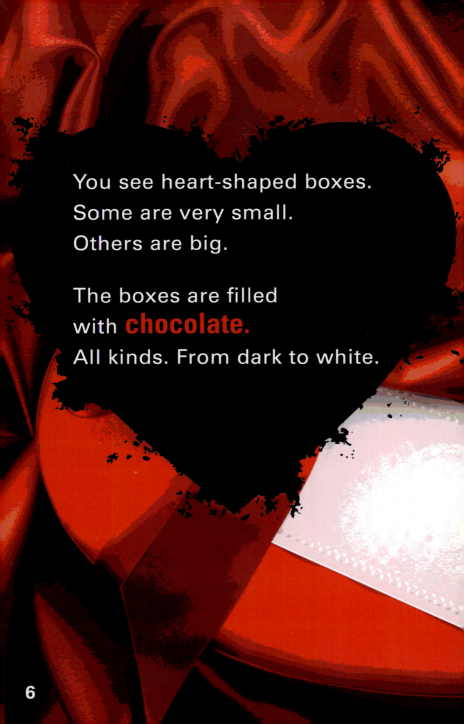

You see heart-shaped boxes.
Some are very small.
Others are big.

The boxes are filled
with **chocolate.**
All kinds. From dark to white.

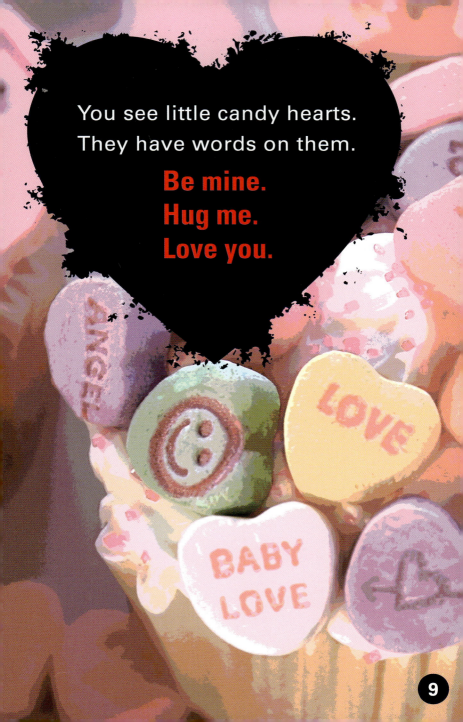

You see little candy hearts.
They have words on them.

Be mine.
Hug me.
Love you.

All these hearts. It can only mean one day. February 14. **Valentine's Day.**

Schools hold parties.
Some have dances.
It is a day for gifts.
It is a day for love.

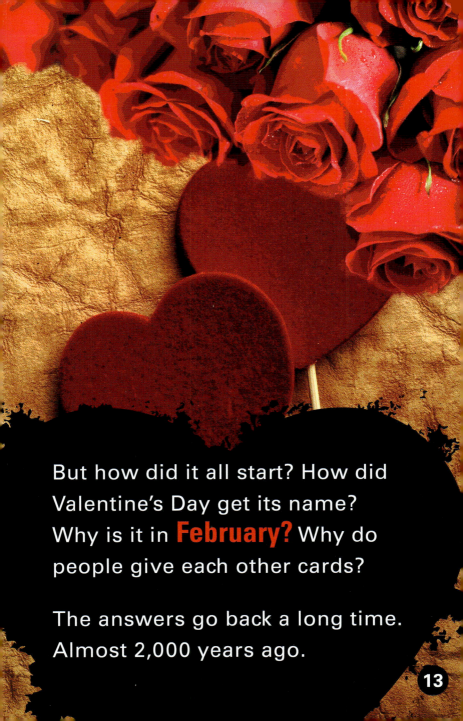

But how did it all start? How did Valentine's Day get its name? Why is it in **February?** Why do people give each other cards?

The answers go back a long time. Almost 2,000 years ago.

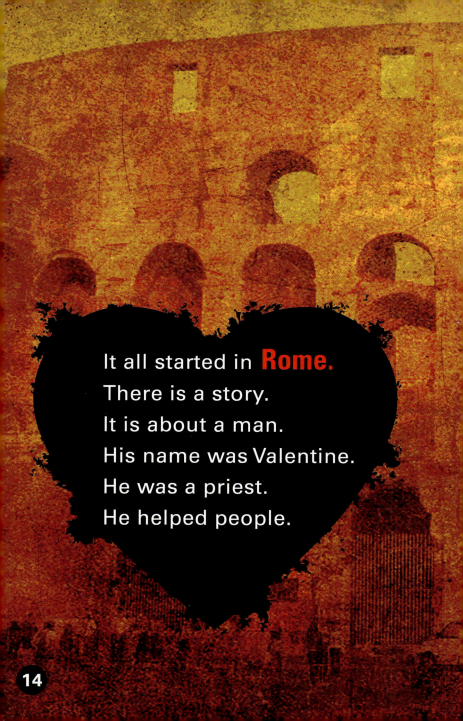

It all started in **Rome.**
There is a story.
It is about a man.
His name was Valentine.
He was a priest.
He helped people.

The leader of Rome had an army. He wanted it to be strong. He wanted young men to be soldiers. Soldiers who would fight for Rome.

The leader thought about his army. He came up with an idea. Men would fight better if they were **single.**

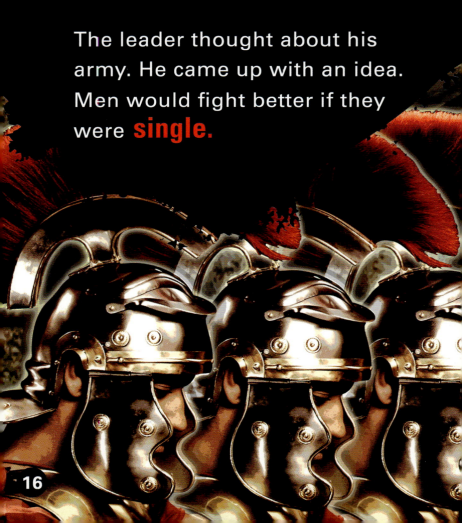

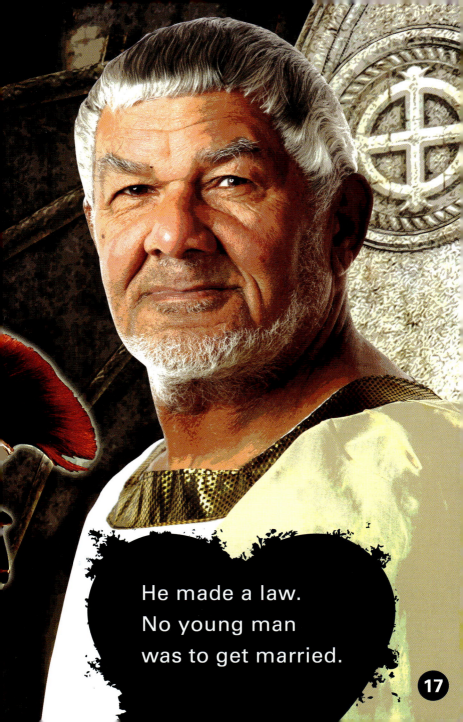

He made a law.
No young man
was to get married.

17

But Valentine did not like this law.
The priest knew young couples.
He knew some who were in love.
They came to him. They wanted
to get **married.**

He helped them.
He broke the law.

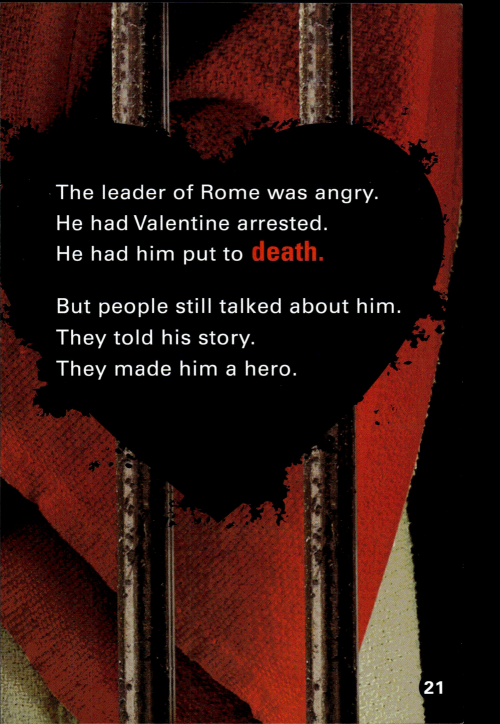

The leader of Rome was angry.
He had Valentine arrested.
He had him put to **death.**

But people still talked about him.
They told his story.
They made him a hero.

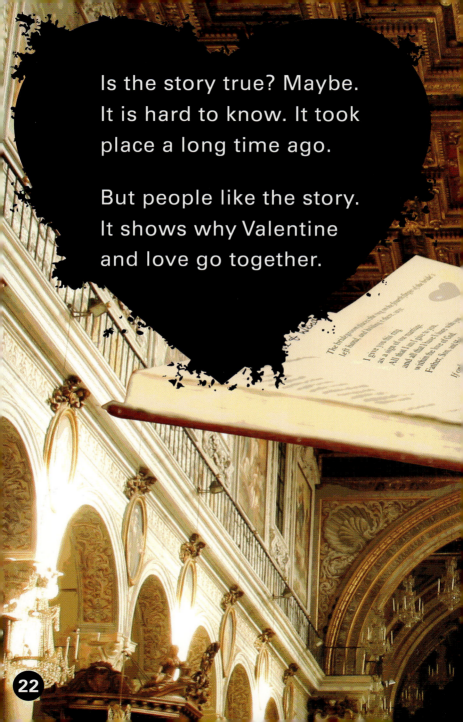

Is the story true? Maybe. It is hard to know. It took place a long time ago.

But people like the story. It shows why Valentine and love go together.

24

There is another story. It is from the same time. It is also about a man named **Valentine.**

This man was a priest too. He helped people who were in jail. Some were hurt badly. He helped them escape.

The priest was caught. Roman soldiers put him in jail. He saw a woman there. Her father watched over the jail. Valentine fell in love with her.

The priest was put to death. But before he died, he wrote a note. He wrote it to the woman. He signed it. It said, **"From your Valentine."**

With Love *from your* Valentine

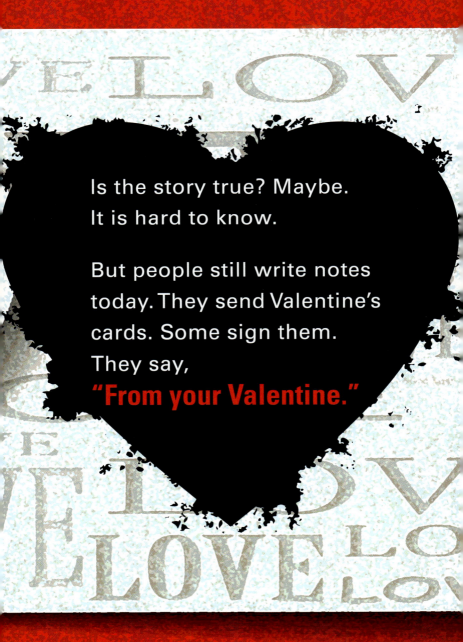

Is the story true? Maybe. It is hard to know.

But people still write notes today. They send Valentine's cards. Some sign them. They say, **"From your Valentine."**

Valentine's Day is in February. Why? It was made to remember the priest. He died because he helped people. What day was he put to death? People think it was **February 14.**

We know when the day was named. It was 496. That is over 1,500 years ago.

Each year people would think of the priest. They would remember what he did. Some would have a feast. They would eat. They would drink.

Over time they did more.
They started to send notes.
They saw it as a **day for love**.

How do we know this? We have books written long ago. One is a poem. It was written in 1382. The poet was **Chaucer.**

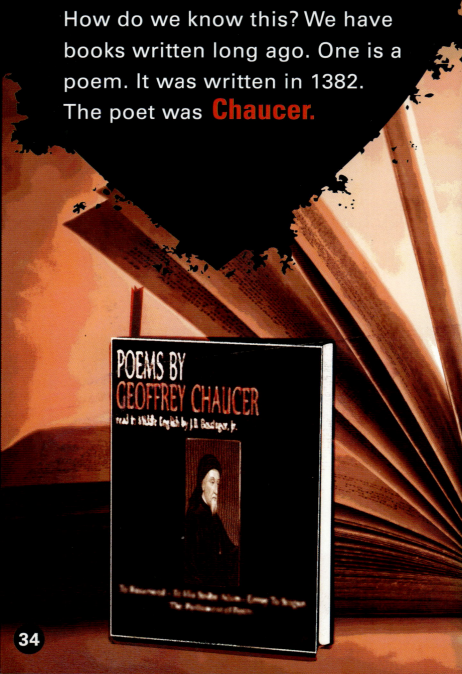

He talks about Saint Valentine's Day. He calls it a day for birds to mate. People heard this. They saw it as love. The day was not just for birds. It was for people. It became a time to send love notes.

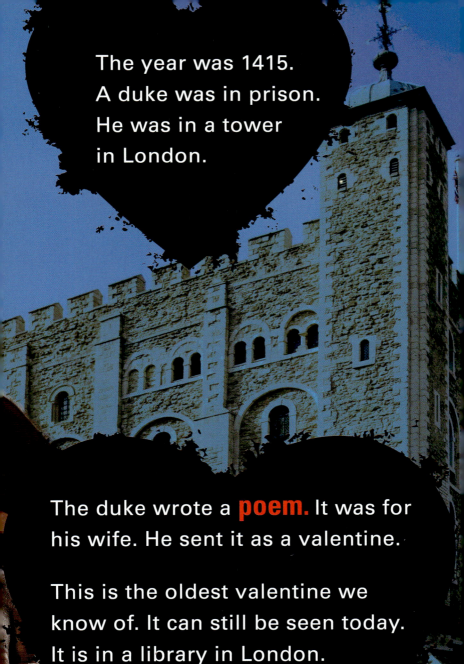

The year was 1415.
A duke was in prison.
He was in a tower
in London.

The duke wrote a **poem.** It was for his wife. He sent it as a valentine.

This is the oldest valentine we know of. It can still be seen today. It is in a library in London.

Valentine's cards got more and more popular. At first, cards were made by hand. People would add **ribbons.** They would add **lace.**

Then things changed. People began making cards to sell. People could buy cards. This took less time. They could give more people cards.

My
Valentine
think of me.

Selling cards made people money. So people made a lot.

A woman did this in 1840. She was the first in the U.S. She made fancy cards. People gave her a name. **"Mother of the Valentine."**

Today, cards are still big business.
People send a lot of valentines.
Over **one billion** each year.

They give them to people
they love.
Husbands.
Wives.
Boyfriends.
Girlfriends.

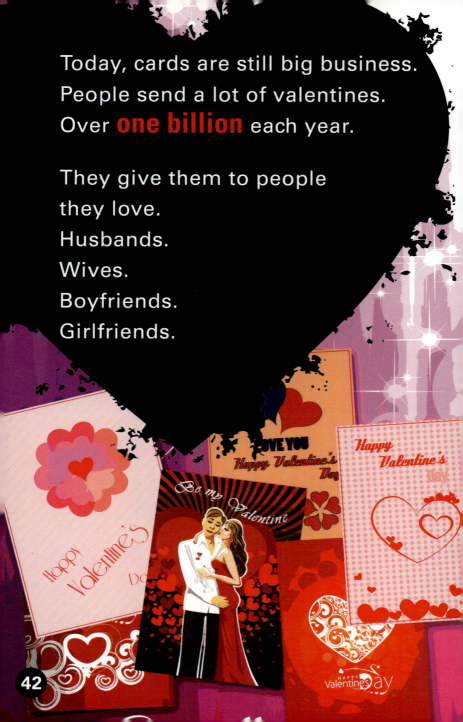

But they also give cards to family. And to friends. And to teachers. Kids give out cards at school. People send cards in the mail.

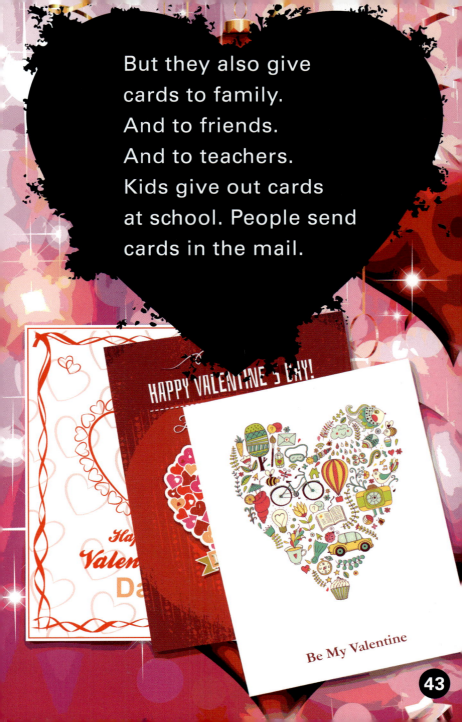

HAPPY VALENTINE'S DAY!

Ha Valen Da

Be My Valentine

Many cards come with gifts. What is the most popular Valentine's gift? Candy. And chocolate most of all.

Chocolate has been around a long time. But it was hard to get at first. And it tasted bitter.

That changed in the 1800s. The first chocolate bar was made. People liked it a lot.

One man had a company. His name was **Richard Cadbury.** The company made chocolate candy. It wanted to sell as much as it could.

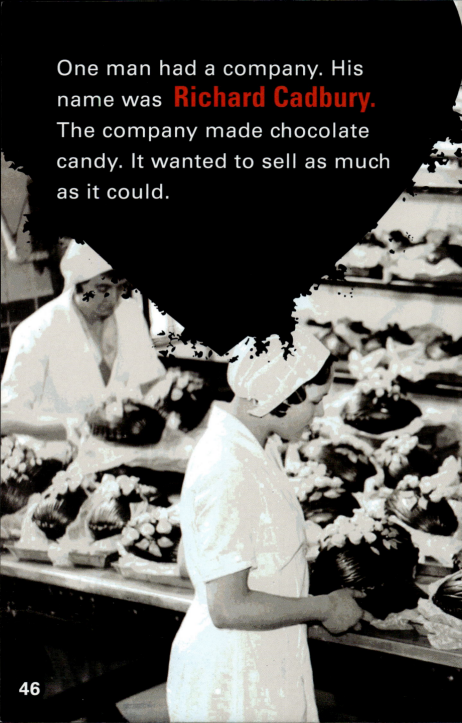

Cadbury had an idea. He put chocolate candies in a box. The box was shaped like a heart. He sold it for Valentine's Day.

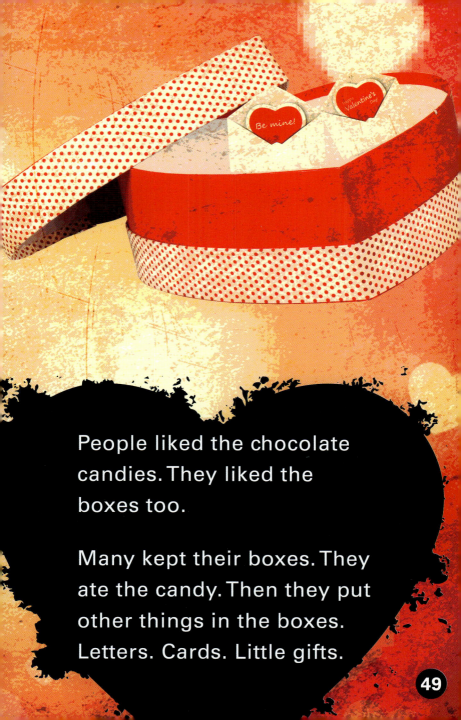

People liked the chocolate candies. They liked the boxes too.

Many kept their boxes. They ate the candy. Then they put other things in the boxes. Letters. Cards. Little gifts.

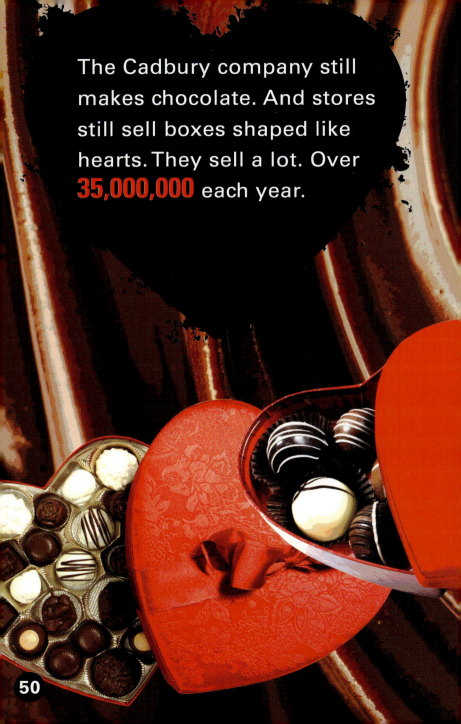

The Cadbury company still makes chocolate. And stores still sell boxes shaped like hearts. They sell a lot. Over **35,000,000** each year.

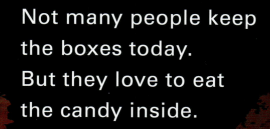

Not many people keep
the boxes today.
But they love to eat
the candy inside.

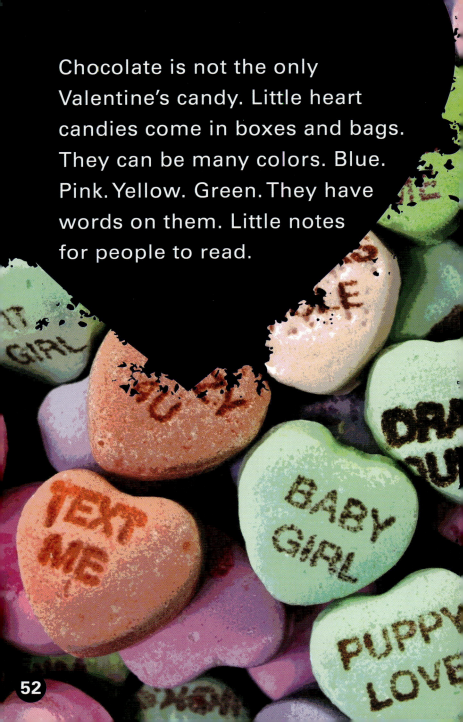

Chocolate is not the only Valentine's candy. Little heart candies come in boxes and bags. They can be many colors. Blue. Pink. Yellow. Green. They have words on them. Little notes for people to read.

These hearts have been around a long time. Over 100 years. Each year a few new words are added. Here are some of the new ones.

Tweet me.
#Love
Recipe 4 Love.

People love to give candy.
Some say, "Sweets for the sweet."
But there are other Valentine's gifts.
Flowers are very popular too.

Which flower do you
see the most? **Roses.**

Each flower has a meaning. The
meaning changes with the color.
Red roses mean love. People use
them to say, "I love you."

The third most popular
gift is **jewelry.**
Necklaces. Rings.
Earrings. Bracelets.
They sparkle and shine.
They make people feel special.

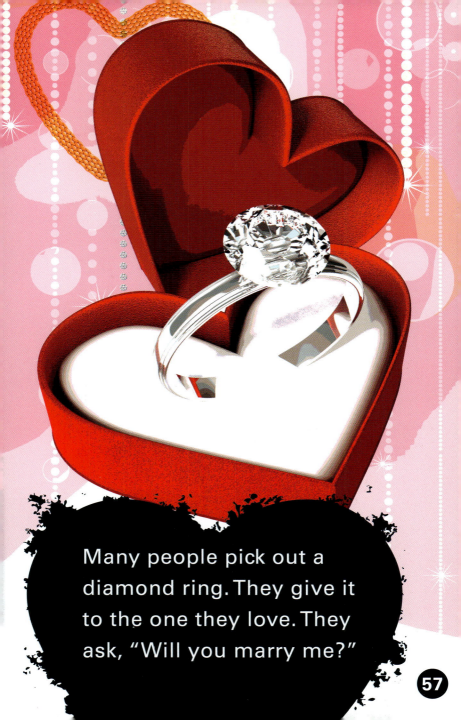

Many people pick out a diamond ring. They give it to the one they love. They ask, "Will you marry me?"

All these gifts are good for stores.
Valentine's Day is big business.
People in the U.S. spend a lot.
As much as $20,000,000,000.

That is why you see big displays. Stores put out cards and candy early. You can find them weeks before the day.

Restaurants like the day too.
Many people go on dates.
They get dressed up.
They go out to dinner.
They eat. They drink.
It is a special day.

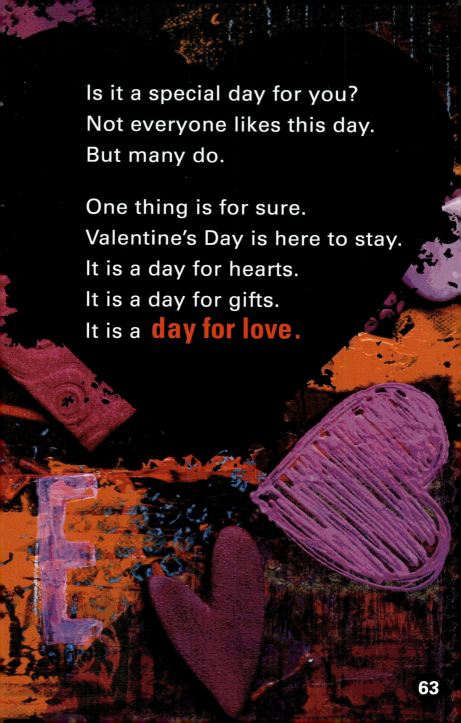

Is it a special day for you?
Not everyone likes this day.
But many do.

One thing is for sure.
Valentine's Day is here to stay.
It is a day for hearts.
It is a day for gifts.
It is a **day for love**.